Note to parents, carers and teachers

Read it yourself is a series of modern stories, favourite characters and traditional tales written in a simple way for children who are learning to read. The books can be read independently or as part of a guided reading session.

Each book is carefully structured to include many high-frequency words vital for first reading. The sentences on each page are supported closely by pictures to help with understanding, and to offer lively details to talk about.

The books are graded into four levels that progressively introduce wider vocabulary and longer stories as a reader's ability and confidence grows.

Ideas for use

- Begin by looking through the book and talking about the pictures. Has your child heard this story before?

- Help your child with any words he does not know, either by helping him to sound them out or supplying them yourself.

- Developing readers can be concentrating so hard on the words that they sometimes don't fully grasp the meaning of what they're reading. Answering the puzzle questions on pages 30 and 31 will help with understanding.

For more information and advice on Read it yourself and book banding, visit **www.ladybird.com/readityourself**

Book
Band
5

Level 2 is ideal for children who have received some reading instruction and can read short, simple sentences with help.

Special features:

Frequent repetition of main story words and phrases

Short, simple sentences

Once upon a time, a little old woman made a gingerbread man. She put him in the oven to cook.

7

Large, clear type

So the gingerbread man jumped onto the fox's tail.

"My feet are wet," said the gingerbread man.

"Jump up onto my back," said the fox.

Careful match between story and pictures

24

25

Educational Consultant: Geraldine Taylor
Book Banding Consultant: Kate Ruttle

A catalogue record for this book is available from the British Library

Published by Ladybird Books Ltd
80 Strand, London, WC2R 0RL
A Penguin Company

006

ISBN: 978-0-72327-288-5

Printed in China

The Gingerbread Man

Illustrated by Virginia Allyn

Once upon a time, a little old woman made a gingerbread man.

She put him in the oven to cook.

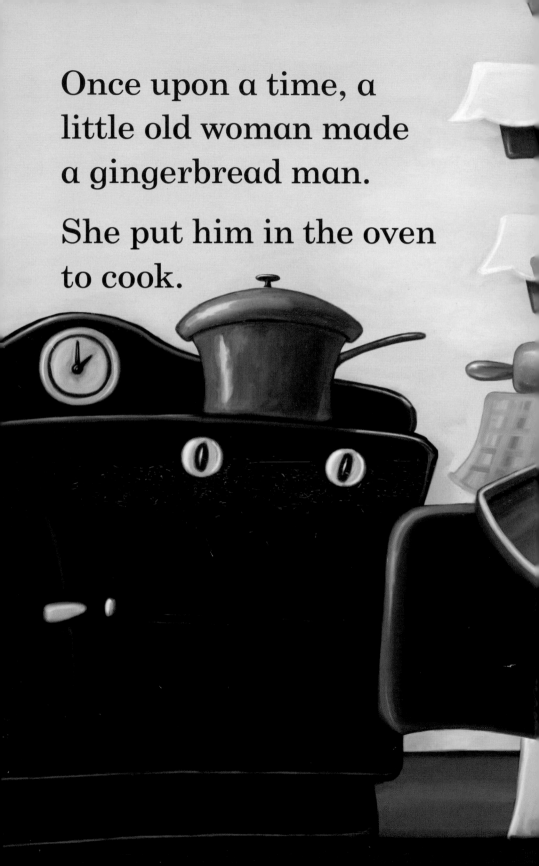

Soon, the gingerbread man was cooked. The little old woman took him out of the oven.

The gingerbread man jumped up and ran out of the door.

9

"Stop, little gingerbread man!" shouted the little old woman. "I want to eat you for my tea."

11

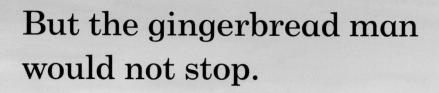

But the gingerbread man would not stop.

The little old woman chased the gingerbread man, but she could not catch him.

Soon, the gingerbread
man met a cow.

"Stop, little gingerbread
man!" shouted the cow.
"I want to eat you for
my tea."

But the gingerbread man
would not stop.

The cow chased the
gingerbread man, but
she could not catch him.

Soon, the gingerbread
man met a horse.

"Stop, little gingerbread
man!" shouted the horse.
"I want to eat you for
my tea."

But the gingerbread man would not stop.

The horse chased the gingerbread man, but he could not catch him.

Soon, the gingerbread
man came to a river.
There he met a fox.

"I will help you to cross
the river," said the fox.
"Jump up on to my tail."

So the gingerbread man jumped on to the fox's tail.

"My feet are wet," said the gingerbread man.

"Jump up on to my back," said the fox.

So the gingerbread man
jumped on to the fox's back.

"My feet are still wet,"
said the gingerbread man.

"Jump up on to my head,"
said the fox.

So the gingerbread
man jumped on to the
fox's head.

Snap! went the fox.

And that was the end of
the gingerbread man.

How much do you remember about
the story of The Gingerbread Man?
Answer these questions and find out!

- Who makes the
  gingerbread man?

- Can you remember
  two of the animals the
  gingerbread man meets?

- Why does the
  gingerbread man
  stop running?

- Who helps the
  gingerbread man
  to cross the river?

Look at the pictures and match them to the story words.

fox

gingerbread man

little old woman

cow

Read it yourself with Ladybird

Tick the books you've read!

For beginner readers who can read short, simple sentences with help.

Level 2

 Beauty and the Beast ☐

 Chicken Licken ☐

 Little Red Riding Hood ☑

 Nature Trail ☐

 Sports Day ☐

 Pirate School ☐

 Rumpelstiltskin ☐

 Sleeping Beauty ☐

 The Gingerbread Man ☑

 Sly Fox and Red Hen ☐

 The Tale of Jemima Puddle-Duck ☐

 The Three Little Pigs ☐

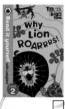 Why Lion Roarrrs! ☐

 The Big Race ☐

 Town Mouse and Country Mouse ☐

 Dom's Dragon ☐

For more confident readers who can read simple stories with help.

Level 3

 YOU won't like this present as much as I DO! ☐

 The Elves and the Shoemaker ☐

 Hansel and Gretel ☐

 Harry and the Bucketful of Dinosaurs ☐

 Jack and the Beanstalk ☐

 Furi on Music Island ☐

 Poppet Stows Away ☐

 Rapunzel ☐

 The Red Knight ☐

 Available on the App Store

The Read it yourself with Ladybird app is now available for iPad, iPhone and iPod touch

App also available on Android devices